On My Own

Written by Jillian Harker
Illustrated by Louise Gardner

Bright Sparks ☆

Deep in the jungle, where only wild things go, Mungo's mom was teaching him what a young monkey needs to know.

"Some things just aren't safe to try alone," she said.

"Why not?" said Mungo. "I'm big enough to do things –

on my own!"

"Now Mungo,"

said Mom, "listen carefully, please. We're going to go through these trees. Stay close to me, and hold my hand. Did you hear what I said?

Do you understand?"

"It's okay, Mom. I won't slip or fall. I can swing across there with no trouble at all," said Mungo.
"I'm big enough to do it—
on my own!"   And off he swung!

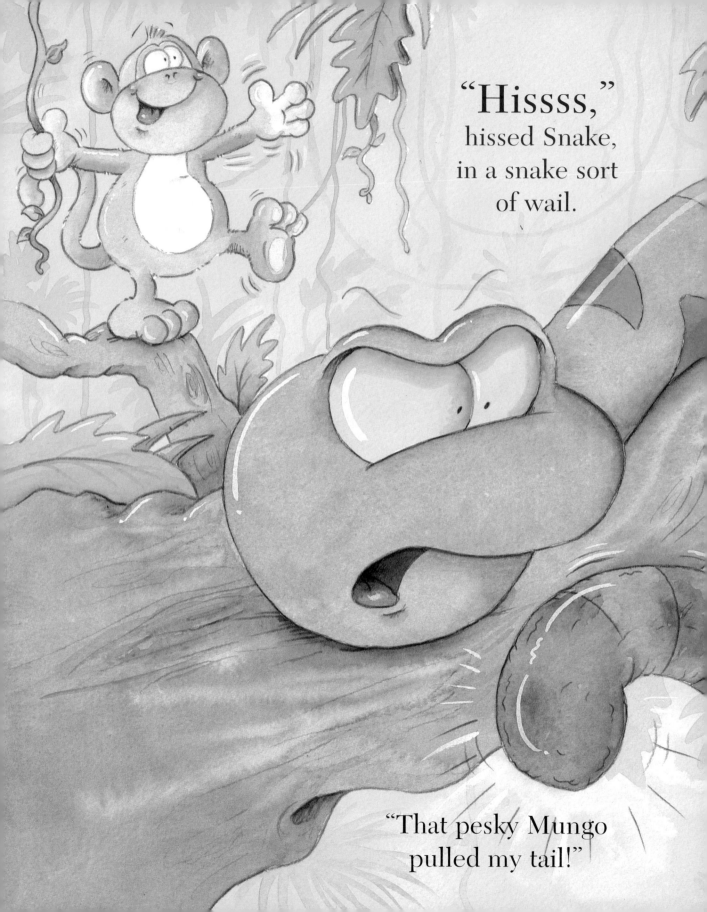

"Hissss,"
hissed Snake,
in a snake sort
of wail.

"That pesky Mungo
pulled my tail!"

And did Mungo hear poor old Snake groan?

No!
Mungo just laughed.
"I told you I could do it
on my own."

"Now, we're going to cross the river by stepping on these stones," said Mom. "But, Mungo, I'd rather you didn't do this alone."

"But Mom," said Mungo, and he ran on ahead, "I'm really good at jumping and hopping. I'm big enough to do it—

on my own!"

And off he sprang!

"That Mungo trampled on my nose!" said Croc.

"Next time, I'll nibble off his toes!"

And did Mungo hear poor old Croc groan?

No! Mungo just smiled. "I told you I could do it on my own."

"Mungo," said Mom, with a serious look on her face, "the jungle can be a dangerous place. There are all sorts of corners for creatures to hide, so, from now on, please stay by my side."

"Oh, Mom," said Mungo, "I don't need to wait for you. I can find my own way through. I'm big enough to do it—on my own!"

Lion rubbed the bump on his nose.

"Ouch!

That Mungo's so careless!" he said.

And did Mungo hear poor old Lion groan?
No! Mungo just grinned. "I told you I could do it
on my own."

"I think I've had enough for one day," Mom said. "So get going, little monkey!

Now it really is time for bed!"

It was Mungo's turn to let out a gr_oan.

"I don't want to go to bed –
on my own!"

"Don't worry," said Mom. "Come on,
kiss me good night, and I promise I'll
hold you and cuddle you tight."

Lion r**o**a**red,** "Is that Mungo still awake?" "**Yes!**" snapped Crocodile.

"Let's help him go to sleep," hissed Snake.

And into the velvety, starry sky drifted
the sounds of a jungle lullaby.